This Little Tiger book belongs to:

_____

_____

_____

For Scarlet, who went to the zoo to see a cow ~ S S
For Leeson, with love x ~ H G

LITTLE TIGER PRESS
1 The Coda Centre,
189 Munster Road, London SW6 6AW
www.littletiger.co.uk

First published in Great Britain 2013
This edition published 2013
Text copyright © Steve Smallman 2013 • Illustrations copyright © Hannah George 2013
Steve Smallman and Hannah George have asserted their rights to be identified as the author
and illustrator of this work under the Copyright, Designs and Patents Act, 1988
A CIP catalogue record for this book is available from the British Library

ISBN 978-1-84895-486-1
LTP/1900/0883/0314 • Printed in China
2 4 6 8 10 9 7 5 3

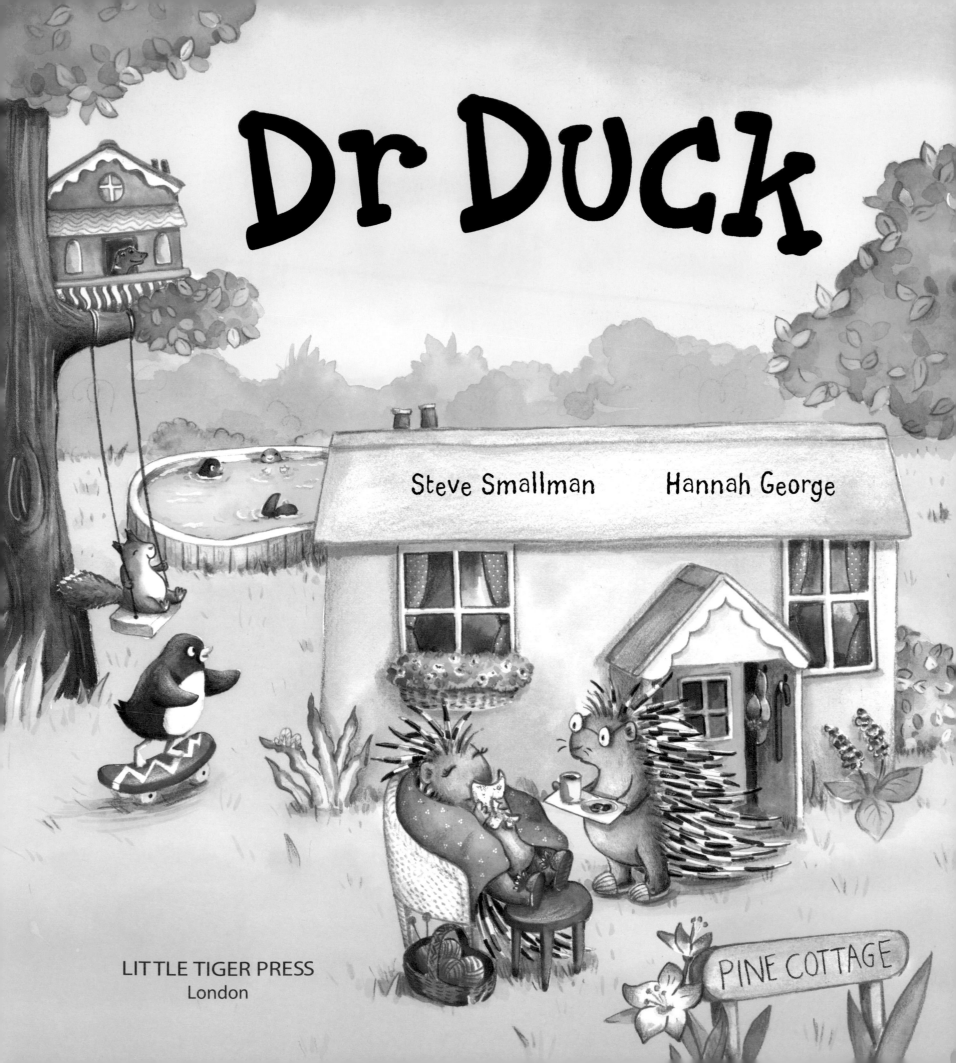

Dr Duck

Steve Smallman   Hannah George

LITTLE TIGER PRESS

London

PINE COTTAGE

Porcupine was poorly, her nose was wet and dribbly,
Her head felt full of cotton wool, her legs were weak and wibbly.
Her nose began to tickle and she gave a **mighty sneeze**,
And with a w h o o o o s h

"A...a...a...chooooo!"

her spines shot off and rattled through the trees.

The zookeeper came rushing in and said,
"What rotten luck!
But don't you worry, Porcupine,
I'll call for...

"DOCTOR DUCK!"

The doctor gave her cactus juice,
to help grow back her spines,
And then two special purple pills
for poorly porcupines.

Giraffe called out, "I'm poorly too,
from standing in the breeze.
It's made my neck go stiff
while I've been nibbling the trees!"

"I've got a temperature!" hissed Snake.
"I'm hot as hot can be!
Oh, Doctor, is there something
in your big black bag for me?"

The doctor put a ladder up
beside the tall giraffe.
Then wrapped the toasty snake
around her neck — just like a scarf!

"Your neck will soon be fine," he said.
"Now, go back to your trees.
And Snake will feel much better
as he cools down in the breeze!"

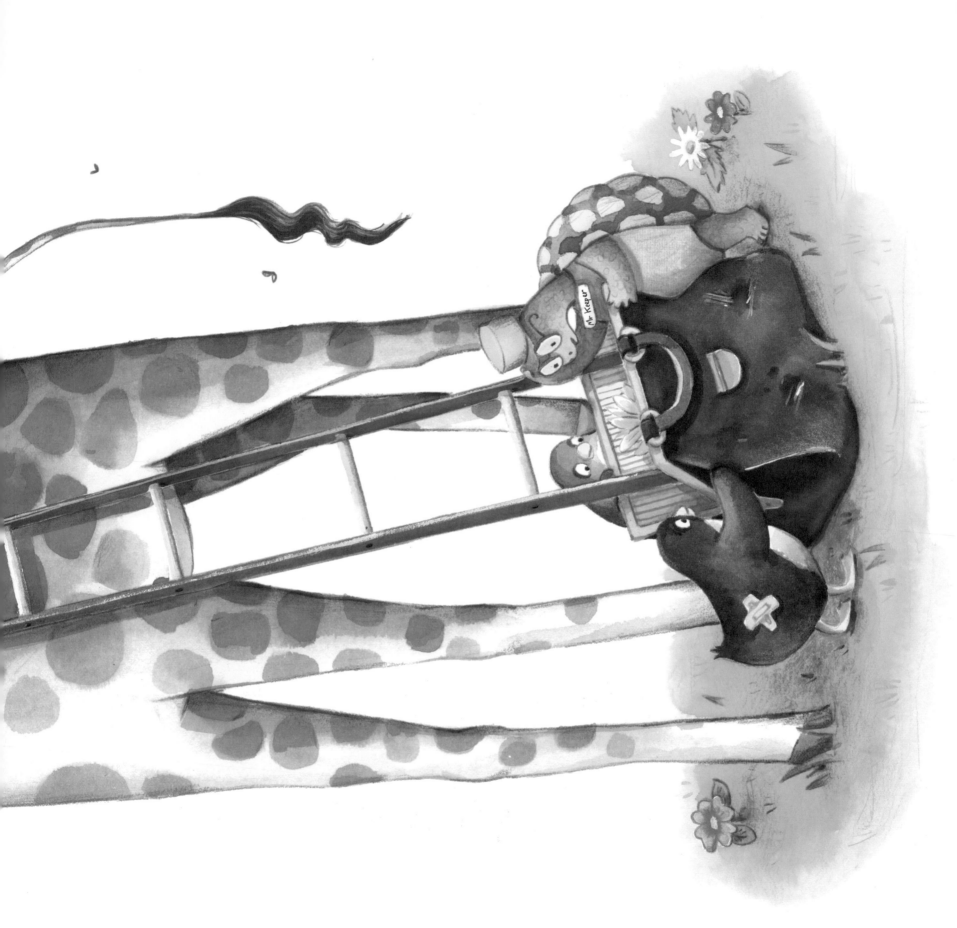

Hyena whined, "Please, help me too!
I'm feeling really glum."

So Doctor Duck tried giving him a tickle on the tum.
He whispered in his ear a joke so silly and so daft,
Hyena started sniggering...

then laughed...

and laughed...

and laughed!

Gorilla shouted, "I've got wind!
  I need some help as well!
I'm tooting like a trumpet and
  I just can't stand the smell!"

"Poo-ee!" gasped Doctor Duck.
"I think this calls for something drastic!
These pants will hold the pong in
with their **extra-strong** elastic."

"Doctor," said the keeper, "you're a genius, it's true!
Porcupine is feeling so much better thanks to you.
Giraffe's neck isn't stiff and Snake is feeling nice and cool.
Hyena can't stop laughing like a wriggly, giggly fool!"

"That's great!" said Doctor Duck.

"Well, I'll be going then, goodbye!"

"No, wait!" cried Mr Keeper.
"Look, what's that, up in the sky?
Is it a bird? Is it a plane?"
"No, no," Hyena grinned...

"I think it's poor Gorilla

with his **knickers** full of **wind!**"

"Oh, no!" said Doctor Duck. "The breeze is blowing him away!
Quick, Porcupine, I need you. Only you can save the day!"
He fetched his feather duster and he gave her nose a tickle.
She sneezed, "Achooo!" and with a whooosh...

Gorilla's pants were punctured
  with a rude and funny sound,
And, trailing clouds of stinky gas,
  he floated to the ground.

"Thank you, Doctor Duck!" said Mr Keeper.

"You're so clever."

And everyone agreed he was

the greatest doctor ever!

"Ooh, don't go yet!" cried Elephant.
"You've got to help me, please!"

"I've got a tickle in my trunk,
I think I'm going to ..."

More fantastically funny books from Little Tiger Press!

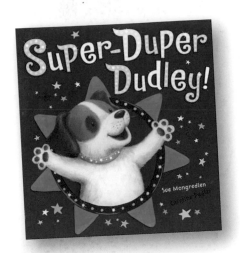

Super-Duper Dudley!
Sue Mongredien

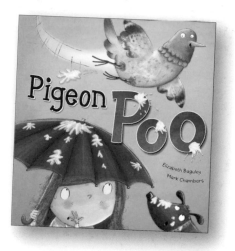

Pigeon Poo
Elizabeth Baguley
Mark Chambers

Dragon Stew

with fold-out pages

My MONSTER DUMPER TRUCK
Steve Smallman
Joelle Dreidemy

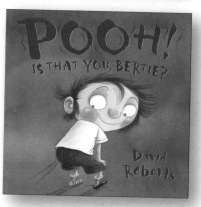

POOH! IS THAT YOU, BERTIE?
David Roberts

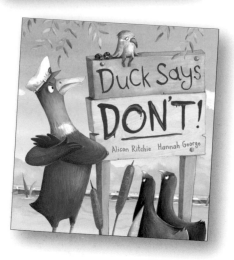

Duck Says DON'T!
Alison Ritchie
Hannah George

For information regarding any of the above titles
or for our catalogue, please contact us:
Little Tiger Press, 1 The Coda Centre,
189 Munster Road, London SW6 6AW
Tel: 020 7385 6333 • Fax: 020 7385 7333
E-mail: contact@littletiger.co.uk
www.littletiger.co.uk